To my family for their inspiration and encouragement.
Blowing special kisses to each of you.

www.mascotbooks.com

Blowing Kisses

©2015 Jaime Windle. All Rights Reserved. No part of this publication may be reproduced, stored in a retrieval system or transmitted in any form by any means electronic, mechanical, or photocopying, recording or otherwise without the permission of the author.

For more information, please contact:
Mascot Books
560 Herndon Parkway #120
Herndon, VA 20170
info@mascotbooks.com

Library of Congress Control Number: 2015911879

CPSIA Code: PRT0915A
ISBN-13: 978-1-63177-283-2

Printed in the United States

Blowing Kisses

Written by
Jaime Windle

Illustrated by
Elisa Moriconi

Did you know

when you blow a kiss…

…sometimes you can add a sweet little wish?

First you kiss the palm of your hand…

…but that's not the last place
your kiss will land!

Close your fingers
to hold it tight…

…and think of a wish
to make it just right.

...but

there is one more thing
you need to know.

Who will you blow
your special kiss to?

There are so many choices but who, just who?

Will it be Mommy or Daddy,
your sister or brother?

Or will it go to a special

"some-other"?

Now that you have picked
your special someone,
there's only a few more steps
until you are done.

Open your hand

and aim it just right…

...now softly blow,

sending

your

kiss

into

flight.

As it soars through the air,

just what do I see?

You blew your kiss over to me!

It lands on my cheek, but that's not the best part,
your kiss with a wish warms my heart!

There's one last thing for me to do...

...softly blow a kiss

right back to YOU!

About the Author

Jaime Windle is a stay-at-home mother of two young children that love to blow kisses. Jaime lives in Vancouver, British Columbia. This is her first children's book.